The Imperfectly Perfect Puppy

The Unbeatable Spirit of Trixie the Bernese Mountain Dog

The Imperfectly Perfect Puppy

The Unbeatable Spirit of Trixie
The Bernese Mountain Dog

Life Lessons from Dogs series

by Joann Neve M. Ed
Illustrated by Janelle Edstrom

Joann Neve

The Imperfectly Perfect Puppy
Copyright © 2021 by Joann Neve

First Edition

Hardcover ISBN: 979-8-9852633-0-5
Paperback ISBN: 979-8-9852633-1-2
eBook ISBN: 979-8-9852633-2-9

Visit the author's website at
J O A N N N E V E . C O M

Also in the Life Lessons from Dogs series:
Make Room for Jasper

The Imperfectly Perfect Puppy will bring a smile! As a therapist, mom and grandma, I always appreciate a story that shares the emotions and challenges of life. Trixie's story teaches us the value of compassion and perseverance to face a disability, fear of the unknown or doubt in our own capabilities. She encourages us to meet the se moments with a little help from our friends and find joy in the journey. Even as we flounder a bit like Trixie, may we all find the beauty and purpose in our very own "Super power".
— Teri Struthers, M.A., LPCC

Trixie's story is one of resilience. Despite her struggles, she is loved and has support for all of her differences. This gives her the courage to keep trying and get more comfortable with things that were scary at first. Many kids can identify with apprehension about trying new things or meeting new people, and watching Trixie gain confidence in her new skills can give them hope that they can achieve the same. Mom identifying Trixie's super power of helping others is another gem, as young children often wish they had super powers, and this reframing of something so inherent in Trixie's personality shows that we all have hidden powers, if only we take a step back and look. Joann has produced another fun story, with an engaging narrative that presents resilience, acceptance and love in a concrete way that children can understand.
— Sara Goudge MA, LPCC, Child/Adolescent Therapist, Mom of three

"Children will grow to love Trixie and root for her as she struggles with being the runt of the litter. My nine-year old daughter said "5 out of 5 stars!" and thought that kids ages 7 through adults age 90 should read the book. Parents will turn the pages as they read to their children and wonder how Trixie overcomes her challenges. This book teaches kids to have empathy for the weak and see the value of those who do not have the abilities of their peers. A great book and must read for those families who want to get a puppy, a dog from a shelter, or foster a dog that has physical challenges -- or for those who just love puppies!"
—Laura Schultz

The Imperfectly Perfect Puppy, (The unbeatable spirit of Trixie, the Bernese Mountain dog) carries an important message for all of us: Despite the challenges we may face, when we are given love and support and encouraged to do our best, our superpowers come through. The story and the illustrations are engaging and endearing and teach children to do their best and also be supportive and inclusive of others. Highly recommended for all children!
— Annmarie Cantrell, M.Ed.

To my pup, Trixie. You teach me everyday that challenges are just part of life, and are not put in our way to defeat us. You never loose your love of life and living. Thank you!

Lotus was an exceptional Bernese Mountain dog, and she was going to have puppies.

Her owner, Robin, was thrilled but calm. This was not the first litter for Lotus. They were ready.

The day finally came and Lotus gave birth to a wonderful litter of nine puppies, six boys and three girls. They were beautiful. Some of the most beautiful puppies you would ever see.

One, in particular, though, was different. Trixie was small—tiny for a Bernese Mountain dog puppy.

She was so small she even needed some help to feed. Robin had to feed her with a bottle for a while.

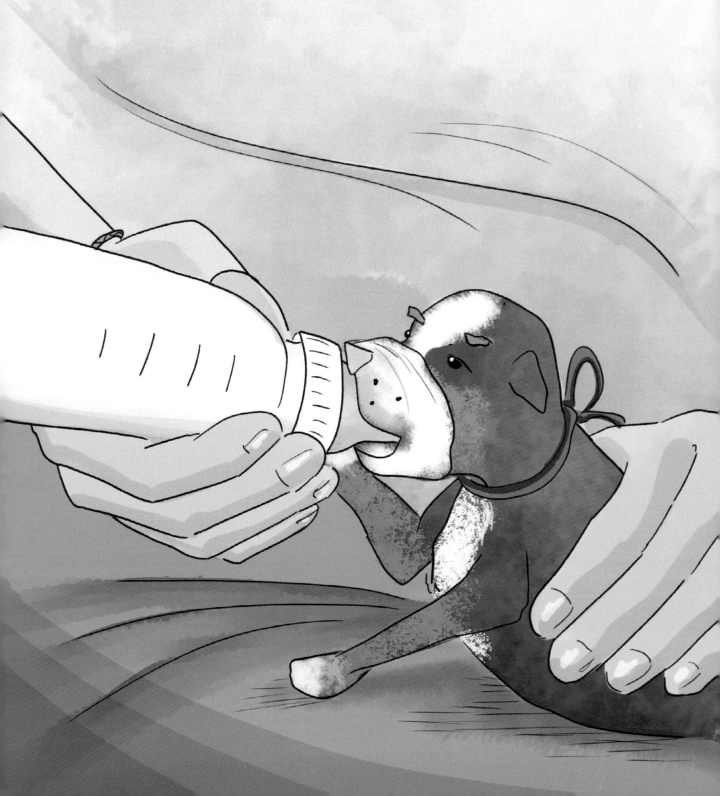

As Trixie grew, it was clear there was something wrong. She was not getting around as well as her brothers and sisters and seemed confused.

The doctor confirmed: "Trixie is blind!"

Robin put Trixie in a separate puppy area so the other pups would not trample her. She gave Trixie stuffed animals to keep her company. And of course, Lotus visited Trixie often.

Robin spent lots of time with Trixie. One day, she took Trixie out of her puppy area and put her on the floor. When Robin would call her name, Trixie happily ran to her and cuddled up against her—happy to be close.

If Robin didn't call her, however, Trixie just lay on the floor with legs outstretched like a stranded turtle, spinning in circles on her belly, frantic to find her.

Robin knew she had to teach Trixie to live a normal life; as much as she was able.

Robin took Trixie to the yard with her brothers and sisters. Trixie learned to listen for them and run to where they were playing.

Robin took Trixie to a play area alone and called for Trixie to find her and follow. Trixie ran with excitement toward Robin.

Trixie became very good at these games and, at times, you could never tell that she couldn't see.

As days went on, Trixie became more confident and loved to play as much as she could with the other pups. She also adored her time playing with Robin.

One day, while playing with Robin, Trixie was running straight for a small tree. Like magic, she stopped short of the tree and sniffed around it.

Was it possible Trixie could see?

YES!

Trixie's sight got better and better; and she did more and more things every day. People loved to watch her enjoy life.

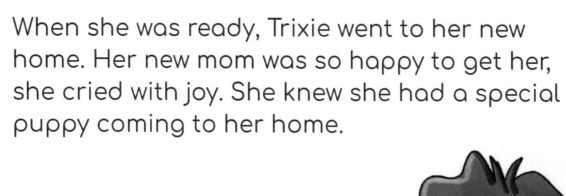

When she was ready, Trixie went to her new home. Her new mom was so happy to get her, she cried with joy. She knew she had a special puppy coming to her home.

Trixie got to go to lots of different places and do new things with her new mom. She also met lots of new dogs.

It was hard at first. No one really knows why Trixie's legs weren't as strong as they should be. They seemed fine to all the experts.

When she would walk, her legs would give out from underneath her. **SPLAT!** She would fall on the floor with all four legs out.

She couldn't get up by herself. She always had to be helped up.

When Trixie would play with other dogs.

SPLAT!

She would fall on the floor with all four legs out.

Trixie would run to greet a dog or person.

SPLAT!

She would fall on the floor with all four legs out.

Trixie also wouldn't go up or down a single stair step. She would never climb or jump on anything.

She was afraid when she had to do anything with her back legs.

Trixie didn't want to use her back legs for **anything!** Even learning how to sit was terribly hard.

Most puppies could learn to sit on command by the time they were very young.

Trixie was so unsure of her back legs, she wasn't comfortable with the sit command until months longer.

But it never changed her spirit and bouncy happiness.

Lying down on command took until Trixie was almost one year old. But it never changed her spirit and bouncy happiness.

Mom never gave up. She continued to work with Trixie on all those little things and never treated her as different.

Getting in and out of the car was very hard. Trixie was too afraid to jump. But it never changed her spirit and bouncy happiness.

Trixie is still learning all she needs to learn, but she had a special talent her mom never realized. Trixie is very kind to all the frightened and lonely dogs she meets. She is very calm and helps them understand everything is OK.

Mom calls that Trixie's **Superpower.**

Trixie is also very good at not getting upset when a dog is mad at her. She stays calm and helps them understand she is not a threat. She makes them feel relaxed so they can listen to their mom and stay calm.

She is called "The Ambassador" at school.

Trixie's life changed a lot since she was a puppy.

She can go down the stairs to play with the other dogs in the backyard. She can jump up on the couch and the bed.

And she can see perfectly.

She is now in obedience training and although it is hard for her, she is doing a great job and never gives up.

She is a happy, energetic puppy who bounces instead of walks, and is ready to take on any challenge. You can see the joy and excitement in everything she does.

Especially when she is hiding one of her favorite "prizes" — a used plastic water bottle or a cardboard paper towel roll.

Trixie does not want to be anyone but who she is.

She is not concerned with what others can do. She is not concerned with what they say she should do.

She enjoys life on her terms and in her own way.

She still has difficulties, and lots more to learn, but she is the **perfect** Trixie.

She is the **imperfectly perfect puppy**.

Now it's your turn to help. Trixie has a lot of things that she will do all in her own happy, special way.

Help her finish her story.

Draw a picture of the fun things Trixie will do next.

CPSIA information can be obtained
at www.ICGtesting.com
Printed in the USA
BVRC090847231121
622224BV00020B/159